★ American Girl®

WITHDRAWN

forever friends

Keiko's Pony Rescue

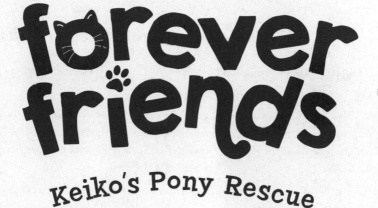

🐾 By Crystal Velasquez 🐾

SCHOLASTIC INC.

To Dax, my best friend's new puppy.
Welcome to the family!
—C.V.

Thank you to the Freier family—Drs. Grace and Dale Freier Jr., Dale III, Mark, Josiah, and Abigail—owners of Every Season Farm, the inspiration for Cherry Blossom Farm. Special thanks to Dr. Heather Wiedrick for her veterinary expertise.

Published by Scholastic Inc., *Publishers since 1920.* SCHOLASTIC and associated logos are trademarks and/or registered trademarks of Scholastic Inc. The publisher does not have any control over and does not assume any responsibility for author or third-party websites or their content.

Book design by Yaffa Jaskoll

ISBN 978-1-338-11495-9

10 9 8 7 6 5 4 3 2 1   18 19 20 21 22

Printed in the U.S.A.   23

First printing 2018

Table of Contents

Chapter 1:
High Hopes

Keiko Hayashi held the fluffy, pint-size dog in her arms.

"Aren't you the cutest thing?" she cooed as she brushed the dog's soft blonde fur out of its eyes. "What should we call you?"

"You should be the one to name her," said Keiko's friend Jasmine Arroyo. "You were the first volunteer to see her when she came in."

The girls were volunteers at Rosa's Refuge Animal Shelter along with their best friends,

1

Sofia Davis and Madison Rosen. Jasmine's mother, Dr. Arroyo, was about to give the dog her first checkup.

"Hmmm," Keiko said. "She's a Pomeranian, right?"

Dr. Arroyo nodded.

"My mom had a Pomeranian when she was a little girl living in Okinawa, Japan," Keiko said thoughtfully. "I know—I'll call her Oki!"

"That's perfect!" Sofia squealed, clapping her hands. "It's so cute, just like her. And she's so tiny, I'm sure she'll be adopted quickly. She'd make such a great pet."

Sofia sighed and looked longingly at the pup. She wanted a dog desperately, but she hadn't been able to convince her parents that she was ready for such a big responsibility.

The other girls smiled at their friend sympathetically.

"Now let's check Oki's vital signs," Dr. Arroyo said.

"Signs? You mean like, 'NO FLEAS ALLOWED'?" Sofia joked, her sense of humor back in a flash.

Dr. Arroyo smiled. "Different kind of sign," she replied. "I'll listen to the dog's breathing, record her temperature and weight, and check her heart rate and rhythm. If those are normal, it's a sign the dog is healthy. I'll write everything down in her chart so we have a record of the exam."

She pulled a pen from the pocket of her white lab coat and wrote down Oki's temperature.

"One hundred and two degrees?" Keiko

cried, reading Dr. Arroyo's note. "Oh no. She has a fever!" Keiko reached out one hand and stroked the dog's fluffy fur, almost expecting it to be hot to the touch.

But Dr. Arroyo shook her head. "Don't worry, Keiko. In humans, a temperature of one hundred and two would be cause for concern, but in dogs, it's perfectly normal. Their body temperature is higher than ours."

Keiko breathed a sigh of relief, tucking her short black hair behind her ears. "Oh good. Because then I would have been so worried about her! And I already have enough to worry about."

Madison looked at Keiko, raising one dark red eyebrow. "Really?" she asked. "What's going on?"

"Well," Keiko replied, taking a deep breath, "I've been too nervous to tell you guys, but I entered an art contest! And I really, really want to win. But I don't know if I will, and it's making me so anxious!"

"That's exciting!" Jasmine said. "What kind of contest?"

"The local art museum is sponsoring it," Keiko explained. "If I win, my drawings will be part of a special exhibit. And then I'll be a *real* artist!"

"Well, of course you'll win," Sofia said, tossing her braids confidently over her shoulder. "And you're already a real artist."

"Sofia's right," Madison agreed, nodding. "You're the best artist in our grade, Keiko."

"Thanks, guys," Keiko replied, blushing.

"But I'm sure a lot of other talented kids entered the contest. Still, I hope I get it!"

"You will," Jasmine said firmly. "So don't even worry about it."

Keiko shrugged, as if she wasn't convinced. "Luckily, I'm leaving soon to visit my aunt's farm for two weeks. That will take my mind off the contest. I leave the day after school ends for summer."

Sofia glanced at Keiko. "That sounds amazing! You'll get to hang out with tons of animals."

"Your aunt has a farm?" Madison asked. "I thought she was a photographer."

Keiko had shown her friends the photographs her aunt had taken of the famous cherry blossom trees in Japan. The photos were so good that they had been displayed in an art gallery in Tokyo. Keiko was proud that her aunt was an artist, just as she hoped to be one day.

"Aunt Yumi *is* a photographer," Keiko answered. "But after she married Uncle Henry, they bought a farm together. They have chickens, cows, pigs, and sheep—and they sell eggs, vegetables, and homemade butter."

"That's so cool," said Jasmine. "You're going to love spending two weeks there."

"Except *we* won't be with you!" Sofia chimed in. "Won't you miss us?"

Keiko nodded. "Of course I will."

Madison propped her elbow on the exam table and slumped down, resting her cheek on her fist. "Your aunt's farm sounds awesome. I wish we could all go."

Keiko gave her friends a big smile. "Why don't you?" she said, her dark eyes lighting up. "I'll have to ask my aunt and uncle, but they love introducing new people to the farm. I bet they'd let me bring a few friends, so long as you agreed to help out."

"Of course we would help!" shouted Jasmine so loudly that Oki yelped and buried her head under her tiny paws. Jasmine winced and scratched Oki behind her ears. "Sorry," she said softly. "Didn't mean to scare you. I just got too excited!" She turned to her mother. "Well, at least we know her hearing is fine! Anyway, could I go with Keiko to the farm for a couple of weeks?"

"I'll have to discuss it with your dad, but I don't see why not," said Dr. Arroyo. "If it's okay with Keiko's parents, and her aunt and uncle, it's okay with me."

"Yes!" shouted Jasmine happily.

"What about you two?" Keiko asked, looking at Madison and Sofia.

Madison smiled brightly. "If my mom says yes, I'm in," she said.

"Me, too," Sofia added. "You guys aren't going on a farm adventure without me!"

Keiko clapped her hands, excited that she might have company on her trip. Visiting the farm would be even more fun with her friends by her side.

Chapter 2
Cherry Blossom Farm

Three weeks later, the girls squished into Keiko's parents' minivan for the two-hour drive to the farm.

"Is there really a pond to swim in?" Sofia asked excitedly.

"Sure is," answered Keiko's mother. "My sister loves the water; that's part of the reason she and Henry chose this farm."

"Sweet!" cried Madison.

Keiko giggled happily. It was great to see her friends so psyched to visit the farm, but no one was more excited than Keiko. Not only would she get to see her aunt and uncle and all the animals, but she'd get to spend time drawing and painting. "I'm going to sketch every day. If I win that contest—"

"You mean *when* you win," Jasmine corrected her.

Keiko shot her friend a grateful smile. "*When* I win, I'll have even more sketches to add to the exhibition."

"We'll help make sure you have time to sketch every day while we're at the farm," Madison said.

Sofia nodded. "I guess we'd better make the

most of these two weeks before you get so busy with your art that you don't have time for us anymore!"

Before the girls knew it, the car turned onto a long dirt road and passed under an arch with a sign that read CHERRY BLOSSOM FARM. There was a beautiful flower on the sign, which Keiko knew had been designed by her aunt. On one side of the road, cows and goats grazed lazily in the sun. On the other, Keiko saw a bright red barn with round bales of hay stacked just inside its open doors. Straight ahead stood a large yellow farmhouse with a wide wraparound porch dotted with small pots of pink flowers. Keiko saw a calico cat perched on the steps, licking her paws and wiping them over her ears, as if she was making herself pretty for guests. It was a picture-perfect scene.

In the center of the porch stood her aunt and uncle, smiling and waving. Aunt Yumi wore faded jeans, a light blue T-shirt, and muddy boots. Next to them was a slightly older woman Keiko didn't recognize. As soon as her father stopped the car, Keiko unbuckled her seat belt, pushed open her door, and ran up the steps. "Aunt Yumi! Uncle Henry!" she gushed.

"Hi, Keiko!" said her uncle. He gave her a quick hug, then stood back to take a closer look at her. "You've gotten so tall!"

Aunt Yumi hugged her and Keiko's parents, too, then greeted the other girls, who were now climbing the stairs. "And these must be your friends," she said.

"Not just friends," Keiko replied. "*Best* friends!" She quickly introduced Jasmine, Sofia, and Madison.

"Any friend of Keiko's is welcome here," said Aunt Yumi. Then she gestured to the other woman on the porch. "This is my friend Grace. She and her husband, Paul, own the farm on the other side of the pond."

"I've heard so much about you," Grace said to Keiko. "I just came by to say hello."

"Looks like you aren't the only one," said Sofia as she glanced at the cat. She was busy sniffing the girls' sneakers and rubbing her furry head against each of their legs.

"This is Sakura," said Aunt Yumi. "That's the Japanese word for 'cherry blossom.' She's named after the farm. Sakura always comes out to meet visitors, don't you?"

Madison reached down to pet the pretty cat, who had an orange spot over one eye and a black patch covering her back. Sakura sniffed at Madison's hand and licked her.

Grace laughed. "Now that I see you girls have been properly welcomed, I should be getting back to Marigold."

"Is Marigold your daughter?" Keiko asked, curious. Maybe there was another girl their age nearby.

"Not exactly," Grace said with a laugh. "Marigold is my pony. I've had her since she was only a few months old. She's expecting a foal soon."

"Ooh!" squealed Jasmine. "I've never seen a newborn foal!"

"Me, neither," said Keiko, Madison, and Sofia at the same time. The girls giggled.

"Well, you may have your chance soon. You're welcome to come by my farm while you're here and meet Marigold."

Not long ago, Keiko would have been too afraid to meet a pony or a horse up close. They were so big, and Keiko used to be afraid of even smaller animals, like dogs. But thanks to the time she'd spent at the animal shelter, Keiko now knew sometimes the largest animals had the biggest hearts. She was looking forward to meeting Marigold. Maybe she could even draw the pony and add the piece to her exhibit—if she won the art contest, that is.

After dinner and a quick tour of the farm, Keiko's parents said their good-byes and headed home, and Aunt Yumi settled the girls in for the night. The four of them had bunk beds in a large upstairs room. Keiko opened the window beside her bed so she could hear the faint moos of cows in the barn and smell the dewy grass of the field.

"Get a good night's sleep, girls," said Aunt Yumi from the doorway. "Tomorrow you'll all be real members of this farm, which means getting up bright and early to help with chores."

"We'll be ready!" Keiko promised.

But the girls were way too excited to go right to sleep. Keiko chose the bed closest to the window. Then she pulled out her sketchbook and sat up against the pillows, drawing a picture of the barn.

"I can't wait to meet all the animals tomorrow," Jasmine said as she flopped down on the top bunk and leaned over to see Keiko's drawing. "Hey, that's really good. I just know you're going to win that contest."

"I hope so," Keiko said softly. She wanted to win so badly.

"You totally will," Madison added. "Can we come to the exhibit?"

"Of course we'll go!" Sofia cried.

"I don't know," Keiko said, suddenly feeling nervous butterflies in her stomach. She wished her friends would stop talking about the contest. It just made it harder not knowing the results yet.

Keiko closed her sketchbook on the

half-finished drawing of the barn and crawled under the covers. "We'd better get to sleep."

Keiko hoped her friends were right about the contest. If they were wrong, Keiko realized she wasn't the only one who would be disappointed.

Chapter 3

Early Birds and a Night Owl

"Wake up, sleepyheads!" Aunt Yumi called as she knocked gently on the girls' door early the next morning. "It's time to get to work."

Keiko opened her eyes, slid out of bed, and peeked out the window. The sun was just starting to rise, and the sky was streaked with red and orange. They would be great colors to add to her barn drawing later.

"Good morning!" Keiko called to her friends.

Sophia groaned as she sat up, stretching. "Didn't we just go to sleep?"

"Not quite," Aunt Yumi said with a laugh.

"I changed my mind about farm life," Madison said groggily. "No one should wake up this early for any reason!"

"I know it's hard at first," Aunt Yumi said. "But you'll get used to it. I thought you might want to feed some adorable baby calves, but if you'd rather sleep in . . ."

Jasmine gasped. "There are baby cows?"

In a flash, all four girls were up and dressed and following Aunt Yumi to the barn. When she swung open the doors, two tiny calves were waiting inside. They had white coats spotted with large black swirls that matched their ears, which stuck out like teacup handles. Every few seconds, they swiped their tongues hungrily over their mouths.

"This is Rosebud," Aunt Yumi said, gesturing to the calf on the right, "and next to her is Lily. They get bottle-fed every day."

"Why don't they drink straight from their mother like kittens do?" Madison wondered aloud.

"They did for the first few days," Aunt Yumi replied. "But now we bottle-feed them so we have enough milk to make butter to sell at the farmers market. Otherwise the calves would drink it all! How would you girls like to help milk their moms?"

Keiko's eyes bulged in surprise. "Us?"

"Yes, you," said Aunt Yumi, smiling. "Don't worry. I'll show you how to do it." Aunt Yumi waved the girls to an enclosure at the end of the barn with two larger cows. They had the same teacup handle–shaped ears and cookies-and-cream coats, but they were much larger than the calves, with long, swinging tails.

"Good morning, Buttercup! How's it going, Lulu?" Aunt Yumi called as she gently patted them.

Aunt Yumi placed a large metal bucket under each cow. Then she sat down on the stool next to Buttercup. "We sometimes use a machine to milk the cows, but today I'll show you how to do it by hand." She stroked the cow's udder, gently squeezing two of the long teats underneath. A moment later, milk began to spurt into the bucket in rhythmic streams.

"That doesn't look so hard," said Keiko confidently. "Can I try?"

"Step right up!" Aunt Yumi replied.

Keiko sat down and carefully wrapped her hand around a teat, just as her aunt had. At first, nothing happened. She angled it toward herself to see if something was wrong and squeezed. *Squirt!* A stream of milk splashed her cheek, making her friends giggle hysterically.

"Lesson number one," said her aunt. "Always aim for the bucket!"

Keiko wiped off her cheek and tried again. Milking the cows wasn't quite as easy as her aunt had made it look, but eventually Keiko got the hang of it. Each of the girls took turns, and soon they had two big buckets full of fresh milk.

"We did it!" Sofia cried.

"Not bad for first-timers," Aunt Yumi agreed, nodding approvingly.

The girls watched as Aunt Yumi poured the milk into bottles and screwed on rubber nipple tops. Aunt Yumi gave one to Keiko. As excited as she was, Keiko felt nervous, too. What if she did it wrong?

She held the bottle cautiously above Rosebud's head, tilting it down toward the calf's mouth. Rosebud quickly latched onto the nipple, pulling on it with soft suckling sounds. Keiko gasped in delight. "She loves it!" she said. Then she handed the bottle to Jasmine so she could take a turn.

"I'm so glad we woke up for this!" cried Madison as she fed Lily.

"Totally worth it," agreed Sofia as she stroked Lily's head.

Keiko smiled at her friends. She was having such a good time getting used to farm life, she had almost forgotten about the art contest!

🐾 🐾 🐾

After they finished feeding the calves, it was time to clean up and have breakfast themselves. As Aunt Yumi and Uncle Henry served the girls plates of fresh scrambled eggs, toast, and fruit, there was a knock at the door.

Aunt Yumi opened it and her neighbor Grace came in, looking worried.

"I'm so sorry to bother you during breakfast, but I need your help," said Grace.

"What's wrong?" Aunt Yumi asked, concerned.

Grace took a deep breath. "My mother is ill, so Paul and I have to fly to Florida tomorrow. But we can't leave Marigold unattended in her condition. I know it's a lot to ask, but would you and Henry be willing to look after her while I'm gone? Our farmhands will take care of most things, but Marigold will need special attention."

"Of course!" Aunt Yumi said immediately. "We'll make sure she's safe and sound."

"Can we help, too?" Keiko asked. She looked around at her friends. "We'd be happy to, right, guys?"

Sofia and Jasmine nodded eagerly.

"Definitely!" Madison agreed.

"That would be wonderful," Grace replied, sighing. "It makes me feel better to know that

Marigold will be in good hands. I'll leave instructions before we go."

That night, her friends went to sleep early, exhausted by their long, exciting first day on the farm. But Keiko stayed up to work on her sketch of the barn. As she finished the last few pencil strokes, she realized she hadn't checked her email since she had arrived on the farm. She pulled out her phone and saw what she'd been waiting for—an email from the museum!

Her heart beating nervously, Keiko clicked on the email. She held her breath as she read:

Dear Keiko Hayashi,

Thank you for your entry in this year's

Amateur Artist contest. Your submission

impressed all the judges! Although . . .

Keiko's heart sank as she read on:

you were not among the winners, you are a

talented artist, and we encourage you to try

again next year.

Keiko couldn't fight her disappointment.
She glanced at her sleeping friends. They had
expected her to win!

Keiko flopped down onto the bed, her face
hot with tears. What would her friends say
when they found out her artwork wasn't going
to be in the museum exhibition after all?

Chapter 4
Henhouse Helpers

The next morning, the girls woke up early—all except Keiko. While the others got dressed, Keiko burrowed into her bed like a hamster and tried to block out the sunlight. How was she going to tell everyone that she hadn't won the contest?

It wasn't until Aunt Yumi finally came and sat on the edge of her bed that Keiko peeked out from under the covers.

"Your friends are already downstairs," Aunt

Yumi said, peering down at her niece with concern. She reached out to touch Keiko's forehead with the back of her hand. "Are you feeling okay?"

Keiko didn't want to worry her aunt, so she untangled herself from the blankets and sat up. "I'm all right," she answered, rubbing her eyes. "I stayed up too late sketching and I guess I needed a little more sleep."

Aunt Yumi returned Keiko's smile. "That's good, because I have an important job for you four today. Get dressed and meet us by the chicken coop. And bring your sketchbook!"

Keiko's aunt hurried out of the room while Keiko changed out of her pajamas. Reluctantly, she grabbed her sketchbook and headed downstairs, trying to think of how she could tell her friends the bad news.

By the time Keiko reached the chicken coop, Jasmine, Sofia, and Madison were already there, each holding a basket.

"About time, Sleeping Beauty!" cried Sofia. "We were starting to think you'd never wake up. Did you stay up late drawing?"

Sofia gestured toward the sketchbook under Keiko's arm.

"Uh, yes," Keiko replied. Then she quickly changed the subject. She wasn't ready to talk about the contest with her friends yet. "Where's Aunt Yumi? She said she had an important job for us."

Madison shrugged. "Your aunt went inside the chicken coop and told us to wait out here for you."

Jasmine swung her basket and grinned. "Maybe we're going to fill the baskets with vegetables to take to Marigold. We finally get to meet her today!"

"Oooh!" Madison squealed hopefully. "I can't wait!"

Suddenly, Aunt Yumi poked her head out of the chicken coop.

"Yes, we'll go see the pony today, but first your chores," she said. "Come on in!"

The girls headed inside, where they were greeted by a chorus of clucking and ruffling feathers. Keiko saw a row of nests, each one with a plump, squawking brown chicken perched on top.

"Ladies, meet the ladies," Aunt Yumi said. "This morning you'll gather their eggs."

She handed a basket to Keiko, who felt her spirits lift a little bit. She'd always wanted to gather eggs!

"Will they just let us take the eggs?" Keiko asked.

In answer, her aunt carefully reached under the nearest hen and pulled out a perfect oval egg. She placed it in Keiko's basket. "See?" she said. "These hens are used to having their eggs taken. As long as you're gentle, they won't mind. Just don't take any eggs from the nest at the end of the row."

The girls glanced at the hen sitting on the last nest.

"Why not?" Jasmine asked.

"Because they're going to hatch soon!" Aunt Yumi announced.

"Yay!" Madison squealed, clapping her hands. "Baby chicks!"

Once Aunt Yumi was sure the girls knew what they were doing, she left them to their task.

"Keiko, look how pretty these eggs are!" said Jasmine sincerely as she placed more eggs in her basket.

Keiko peered down at six delicate eggs nestled there. To her surprise, they weren't all the same color like the eggs her parents bought at the store. Some were white, others were tan or brown or even blueish. They looked perfect against the basket lining.

"You're already thinking about how you would draw them, aren't you?" Jasmine asked with a grin.

Keiko glanced up at Jasmine in surprise. How had her friend known?

"Well, go ahead and start sketching," Sofia said encouragingly. "We'll keep gathering while you create a little masterpiece."

Keiko almost reached for her sketchbook out of habit. But then she remembered the email and stopped, her face clouding over. If she did start drawing, it was only a matter of time before her friends asked about the contest. She shook her head and went back to reaching for eggs and placing them in her basket.

"Thanks, guys," Keiko said, "but I was actually thinking about meeting Marigold. The sooner we finish here, the sooner we can go see her!"

It was a tiny white lie, and Jasmine gave Keiko a strange look, as if she knew something wasn't quite right. But Madison and Sofia quickly went back to gathering eggs, chatting excitedly about meeting the pony.

Keiko put her head down and focused on her work, pushing thoughts of the art contest out of her mind. Maybe if she put her heart into her chores and the animals, the heavy feeling in her heart would go away.

Chapter 5
The Naturals

Later, after the girls had turned in their full baskets, they waited on the porch while Aunt Yumi stored the eggs. She came out of the house, wiping her forehead with her bandanna.

"Phew!" she said with a smile. "You girls did a great job in the chicken coop. You didn't break any of the eggs, and you finished so quickly! Thank you."

"What can we say?" Sofia replied with a shrug. "We're naturals."

Aunt Yumi laughed. "No argument here. Now let's see if you're as great with ponies as you are with hens. I brought some snacks from the garden." She held up a sack filled with carrots that had been cut into small pieces. "Let's go visit Marigold!"

After a long walk down the road and past the pond, they arrived at Grace's farm and headed straight for the stables. In the first stall they found a beautiful pony with a shiny chestnut coat and big, dark eyes. She greeted them with a soft nicker and a swish of her tail.

"She's so pretty!" cried Keiko.

"Can we pet her?" asked Jasmine.

Aunt Yumi stepped forward and pointed to a note tacked to the front of Marigold's stall.

"Hold on a second," she said. "Let's read Grace's instructions first."

Madison, who was working hard to improve her reading, volunteered to read the list out loud. *"One: Marigold likes to be brushed every day and go for walks around the p-paddock. Light exercise is good for her and the baby. Two: Healthy snacks are okay, but don't overdo it. Three: Make sure she has enough hay to eat and plenty of water. Four: Most im-important, give her lots of love and attention."*

"That sounds easy," said Sofia. "Maybe I should stop begging my parents for a dog and ask for a pony instead!"

Keiko giggled. "I'm pretty sure you don't have room for a pony at your house, Sofia," she said.

Jasmine turned concerned eyes to Aunt Yumi. "But what happens if the baby comes before Grace and her husband get back?"

Aunt Yumi took a closer look at the note in Madison's hands. "She left the number for her veterinarian just in case. In the meantime, why don't you all make friends with Marigold. That way, if she does give birth while her owners are away, she'll be comfortable with you and won't be overprotective of the foal."

"Let's start right away," Keiko said. She pulled a carrot from the bag and slowly approached Marigold, holding out her hand. Marigold sniffed at Keiko with her long muzzle and then gently took the carrot from her palm and started chomping.

"Wow, Keiko!" said Jasmine. "Good job."

"You girls really are naturals," Aunt Yumi added.

Keiko beamed as Marigold finished her carrot, then affectionately nuzzled her velvety nose against Keiko's cheek. "I think I have a new friend!" Keiko declared.

When they got back to Cherry Blossom Farm a few hours later, Madison turned to Keiko. "Even after everything we did today, you still have time to draw, Keiko," Madison said.

Keiko's stomach twisted. Meeting Marigold had made her forget all about the contest. Drawing was the last thing she wanted to do.

"That's a great idea," Aunt Yumi said. "I can show you girls the pond. The light will be terrific there at this time of day. And the rest of you can take a dip while Keiko sketches if she wants."

"Oh, she wants to," Jasmine said, smiling knowingly. "Keiko told us she's going to draw every day she's here."

"That's wonderful," Aunt Yumi said, squeezing Keiko's shoulder.

"Uh, um . . ." Keiko muttered, looking down at her shoes. She knew she should just tell her aunt and her friends about the contest, but she couldn't seem to get the words out. "It's, uh, it's a little too hot and sticky for drawing, isn't it? I'd rather swim."

"Yeah, let's go swimming!" Sofia shouted enthusiastically.

After the girls had changed into their bathing suits, Aunt Yumi walked them to the pond.

They swam and splashed until dinnertime. No one mentioned drawing again, and Keiko had fun, but she couldn't shake the sinking feeling in her stomach. She knew she had to tell her friends the truth about the contest sooner or later.

Chapter 6
Marigold in Trouble

For the next few days, the girls began each morning by milking the cows, feeding the chickens, pulling weeds from the vegetable garden, or helping Aunt Yumi make butter. Then they gathered some apples and carrots and headed over to Grace's farm to see Marigold.

Aunt Yumi and Uncle Henry showed the girls how to groom, feed, and walk the beautiful mare. Aunt Yumi explained that the heavy brush used on Marigold's coat was called a currycomb. Then she showed the girls another brush that they could use to untangle and clean the pony's mane and tail.

Keiko had started reading about ponies, too. Her aunt had a collection of books about farm animals. Instead of sketching before bed, Keiko had spent the last few evenings learning more about ponies and horses.

In just a few days, Marigold had become more affectionate around the girls. When the pony saw Keiko coming, she would whinny hello and press up against her pen until Keiko fed her a treat and petted her long neck.

But today, when they entered the barn with Aunt Yumi, the pony acted differently. She didn't greet Keiko at all, and she seemed restless.

"Hey, girl," Keiko said as she showed the pony a small apple. "I brought you a snack."

Usually, Marigold would sniff at Keiko's hand and then gobble up the treat. But today, she paced the stall, her tail flicking wildly. Every few minutes she snorted and stamped.

"What's wrong?" asked Jasmine. "She's usually so happy to see us."

Aunt Yumi frowned. "I'm not sure. Maybe she's thirsty. Her coat looks sweaty—"

Suddenly, Keiko remembered something. "You guys!" she said excitedly. "I just read about this last night! Pregnant ponies and horses act restless like this before they give birth. I think Marigold is ready to have her baby!"

Jasmine gasped. "Right now? What do we do?"

"You're the daughter of a veterinarian," Sofia said, shrugging. "You tell us!"

"That's different," Jasmine said, looking worried. "My mom works with cats and dogs. Unless Marigold is about to have puppies, I don't have a clue!"

Madison pointed to the note Grace had written, which was still tacked to the wall. "Grace left the name and number of her veterinarian. Let's call him."

"Already on it," said Aunt Yumi, who had her cell phone pressed to her ear.

Once the call had been made, there was nothing for Aunt Yumi and the girls to do but wait. Finally, Dr. Brooks arrived. He had brown hair and kind brown eyes, and was wearing rubber boots and a flannel shirt. He had a stethoscope slung around his neck. He went right into the stall while Keiko and the others waited outside.

"I hope she's okay," said Jasmine.

"Me, too," Keiko replied.

Dr. Brooks used the stethoscope to check Marigold's heartbeat.

"Sounds good," he told them. Then he pulled on a pair of gloves.

"Now I'm going to give her an exam to see how far along her labor is," he explained.

"Wow!" cried Jasmine. "You were right, Keiko!"

Keiko nodded, a serious look on her face. She waited impatiently for the doctor to finish checking Marigold.

"Is she going to be okay?" she asked Dr. Brooks as he peeled off the gloves.

He nodded. "Once a mare is in labor, she usually prefers to be left alone to do what comes naturally," he explained. "I'll stay to monitor the process, but it could take hours."

"I have to know whether Marigold and her baby are okay," Keiko said. She turned to her aunt. "Can I stay until the baby is born? *Please?* I want to help."

Aunt Yumi's eyes softened. "I understand. I

want to help, too. But I'm not sure there's much any of us can do."

"We can at least be close so Marigold knows we're here for her," Keiko replied.

"Yeah," said Sofia, nodding.

"I want to stay," Jasmine added.

"Me, too!" Madison said.

Aunt Yumi exchanged a glance with Dr. Brooks, who nodded. "All right," she said, "you can stay. But if you're staying, so am I. And if we're camping out, then we're going to do this right!"

Chapter 7
Barnyard Slumber Party

That evening, Keiko, her friends, and her aunt settled into the empty stall across from Marigold's with everything they needed for a proper barnyard sleepover: sleeping bags, blankets, snacks, and a battery-operated lantern. Dr. Brooks sat nearby, reading a book while he waited.

"Are you sure there's nothing else we can do for Marigold?" Keiko asked as she watched the pony nervously.

Aunt Yumi shook her head. "You heard Dr. Brooks. Marigold needs space right now."

Keiko glanced at Marigold's stall and sighed. "I know you're right. I just feel so helpless."

"I know," Jasmine agreed. Then she grinned and reached into her backpack. A moment later, she pulled out a charcoal-gray pencil and Keiko's sketchbook. "But maybe there is something you can do. I saw this on your bed and thought I would bring it. I hope you don't mind. Since Grace can't be here for the birth, I thought maybe you could draw her a picture. Then she'll feel like she was here!"

Keiko hesitated before she reached for the sketchbook. Just looking at it reminded her about losing the contest, and her stomach twisted. Her friends would be so disappointed in her when they heard she hadn't won.

"I—I don't know, Jasmine," Keiko said slowly as she tried to think of an excuse. "It's a little too dark in here, even with the lantern."

Jasmine looked at her friend closely.

"Is everything okay?" she asked. "You haven't been sketching much, and we promised to help you find time for it."

"Yeah!" Madison added, smiling brightly. "We're your personal cheerleaders, remember?"

"I just don't feel like sketching tonight, okay?" Keiko said softly. "Maybe I'll draw something tomorrow." She didn't want her friends to feel bad. After all, Keiko *had* asked them to help her make time to draw. But that was before, when she was sure she had won the contest.

Aunt Yumi, overhearing the conversation, held up the camera she'd brought with her. "Don't worry, I've got Grace covered. I'll take pictures so she won't miss a thing. Now we should probably get some sleep."

The girls settled their sleeping bags into the hay and climbed in. Keiko kept her eyes on Marigold.

"I'm staying up until the baby comes," she announced.

"Me, too," her friends agreed eagerly.

Aunt Yumi chuckled quietly. "Girls, this might take a very long time. The foal may not even come until tomorrow."

"Then we'll stay up all night!" Jasmine declared.

But one by one, Keiko's friends drifted off, and so did Aunt Yumi. After everyone else was asleep, Keiko had a change of heart. She reached for her sketchbook and pencil.

Letting her memory guide her, Keiko drew a picture of Marigold with her glossy coat and long flowing mane. Just putting her pencil to paper again made her feel a little bit better. Maybe tomorrow after the foal was born, she thought to herself, she would get up the courage to tell her friends about the contest.

🐾 🐾 🐾

"Keiko? Wake up, sweetie," a voice called gently.

Keiko shot up. The first morning light streamed in through the barn door. Her friends were snuggled into their sleeping bags, sleeping soundly. Aunt Yumi smiled down at her.

"Is Marigold okay?" Keiko asked, her heart racing. When had she fallen asleep? She hadn't meant to.

Aunt Yumi's smile grew wider. "Marigold is fine. There's someone I think you'll want to meet. It's a girl!"

The foal! Hurriedly, Keiko shook the others awake. "You guys, get up! The foal is here!"

Jasmine was the first to scramble out of her sleeping bag, followed by Sofia and Madison. Together they raced to Marigold's stall and squealed with delight. Marigold was on her feet with her head down. And right by her side, lying on the ground with her legs folded beneath her, was a newborn foal.

"She's beautiful!" Keiko sighed.

Madison clapped her hands. "Aww . . . she's so cute. Look at her fluffy coat! And she has a white mark on her nose, just like her mother."

Marigold was grooming her newborn filly with her tongue, cleaning every inch of the foal from her head to her hoofs. For a while, no one said a word.

Finally, Dr. Brooks eased into the stall. "Time for your first checkup, little lady," he said to the foal.

Jasmine, Madison, Sofia, and Keiko watched as Dr. Brooks carefully examined the newborn.

"It's been a couple of hours now, so the foal should be standing," he explained to the girls. "I'm going to gently help get her on her feet so she can have her first meal."

Keiko watched in awe as Dr. Brooks wrapped the foal in a gentle hug and lifted her up. To Keiko's relief, the foal got her skinny legs under her and stood, looking a bit wobbly. Even though she had read about it in one of Aunt Yumi's books, Keiko was still surprised to see the foal standing on her own so soon after her birth.

Dr. Brooks helped the newborn make her way to Marigold and begin nursing.

"Good girl, um . . ." Dr. Brooks turned to Aunt Yumi, his eyes twinkling. "What should I call this foal?"

"Well, what do you say, girls—shall we give her a name?" Aunt Yumi replied. "Grace won't mind."

Keiko looked down at the filly, who was attached to Marigold like a flower petal to a stem. "Why don't we name her Daisy?" she suggested.

Madison, Sofia, and Jasmine agreed that Daisy was the perfect name for the little pony.

Chapter 8

Keiko's Confession

As soon as the girls had packed up their sleeping bags, they reluctantly headed back to Cherry Blossom Farm to help with the morning chores. Aunt Yumi promised they could come back right after breakfast to get a full report on the ponies from Dr. Brooks.

The girls did their chores hurriedly and then quickly ate the plates of pancakes Uncle Henry had made for them. Then they rushed back to Grace's farm.

"There's good news and bad news," Dr. Brooks told them in greeting.

"What's the good news?" Keiko asked.

"Daisy is a healthy eighty pounds with a great appetite," he answered, giving them an amused grin. "And Marigold is tired, but she's doing just fine."

Keiko breathed a sigh of relief.

"Then what's the bad news?" Jasmine asked nervously.

Dr. Brooks raised his eyebrows, his forehead wrinkling. "Daisy was born with tendon problems in her legs."

"What does that mean?" asked Madison, a worried look on her face.

"Newborn foals are usually able to get around within a few hours, but it's been more than that, and she still isn't walking. Her leg tendons are contracted, which means her front legs are too straight and at the wrong angle for walking. It's a common problem, but if it isn't corrected, she may need surgery."

"Surgery?!" Keiko gasped. "Oh no."

Aunt Yumi's forehead wrinkled with worry. "That *is* bad news," she agreed softly. "Surgeries are expensive, and Grace has enough on her mind with her mother being ill."

Keiko looked at the foal carefully. She was glad to see Daisy standing next to her mother and resting her head against Marigold's belly. But she could also see what Dr. Brooks meant about her front legs. They looked stiff, at odd angles.

Keiko was worried about the little filly. "What can we do to help?" she asked.

"I'll put splints on the legs to hold them in the correct position for about eight hours each day," Dr. Brooks explained. "Then Daisy will need to do some carefully controlled exercises." He glanced at Keiko, Jasmine, Madison, and Sofia. "Do you girls think you could help with that?"

"Yes!" they cried in unison. Keiko knew she and her friends would do whatever they could to help Daisy.

The next morning was Saturday, and Uncle Henry had invited the girls to go with him to the farmers market to sell Cherry Blossom Farm's eggs, butter, flowers, and vegetables, while Daisy was being treated by Dr. Brooks. Uncle Henry set up his table, and the girls helped stock it with blocks of butter, cartons of eggs, and baskets of vegetables and small bouquets of flowers. Keiko was fascinated by the things for sale at the other booths, like goats' milk, cheeses, bunches of lavender, fresh honey, and homemade jams.

"Look, Keiko!" Jasmine said as she arranged the flowers at the front of the Cherry Blossom Farm table. "It looks like a painting."

Keiko agreed—the arrangement of pink and yellow wildflowers was beautiful. As Keiko gazed at the flowers, thinking she'd like to draw them, her shoulders slumped.

"What's wrong?" asked Jasmine. "Are you worried about Daisy? I am, too."

Keiko shook her head. It's true that she *was*

65

worried about Daisy. And suddenly that made the art contest seem less important—and telling her friends about it less scary.

"Yes," said Keiko, "but it's not just that." She paused. "There's something I haven't told you guys."

"What is it?" Sofia asked.

Keiko hesitated.

"You can tell us," Madison said gently. "We're your best friends, remember?"

Keiko took a deep breath. "I didn't win the art contest," she blurted out.

"I'm so sorry," Madison said. "I know how much you were hoping to win."

"Yeah, that's a bummer," Sofia said sympathetically. "Is that why you haven't been drawing much lately?"

Keiko nodded. "I'm really sorry I let you guys down."

"What are you talking about?" Jasmine asked, surprised. "You haven't let anyone down. We think you're an awesome artist!"

"But you were all so excited to see my paintings at the museum," Keiko replied, biting her lip. "Now that will never happen."

"Are you kidding?" Sofia asked. "Of course it will! Just because you didn't win *this* contest doesn't mean your art will *never* be in a museum."

"Sofia's right," Madison said as she put her arm around Keiko. "You may not be a famous artist yet, but you will be, someday. You can't give up on yourself—or your art—after just one contest."

Keiko felt relief flooding through her. She was glad she had finally told her friends the truth. They weren't disappointed in her at all! They still believed in her just as much as before. And, Keiko realized, their support helped her feel more confident about her artwork.

"You need cheering up," Jasmine said. "Let's shop for gifts for Marigold and Daisy!"

"That's a great idea," said Uncle Henry, who had overheard everything. "Once we're done selling, we'll do some buying."

By the time they left the market, the girls had selected a small bag of oats and a few ripe red apples for Marigold and a soft brush especially for Daisy.

Keiko smiled at her friends. Just telling them about the contest had made her feel so much better. Now her biggest worry was Daisy. Would the foal ever learn to walk?

As soon as the girls got back from the farmers market, they headed over to Grace's farm with Aunt Yumi to see the ponies. Keiko rushed to Daisy's stall to find the filly standing awkwardly, splints attached to her front legs. They looked like large bandages.

"Are you girls still prepared to help Daisy?" Dr. Brooks asked.

"Definitely!" Keiko said eagerly. "Just tell us what to do."

The doctor demonstrated a few safe ways to encourage the foal to walk back and forth across the paddock just outside the barn.

"Be gentle but firm," he explained. "She

might refuse to move at first. But it's important to get Daisy to walk as much as possible to strengthen her muscles. Let her lean against you if she needs to, but try to get her to keep walking unless you think she's really in pain. I'll be back to check on her soon."

🐾 🐾 🐾

After Dr. Brooks had left, Keiko looked at her friends. "Let's do this!"

Gently, Keiko pulled on the lead around Daisy's neck as Dr. Brooks had demonstrated. But the foal wouldn't budge.

"How is Daisy supposed to get exercise if she won't move?" Keiko wondered aloud in dismay.

"I don't know," Jasmine replied, her face full

of concern. "But Dr. Brooks said she might refuse at first."

"There's got to be something we can do to encourage her," Madison said thoughtfully. "I just don't know what it is."

The friends were quiet for a minute. They were stumped. Keiko didn't want to force Daisy to walk, but she and her friends knew that if the filly didn't get the exercise she needed, she might need surgery. That would be hard on Daisy *and* on Marigold and Grace, too. Aunt Yumi had explained that doing surgery on ponies was very expensive, and healing was difficult. How could they get Daisy to walk?

Chapter 9
A Winning Plan

That evening, the girls filed into their room and got ready for bed. But none of them could sleep. All they wanted to do was talk about Daisy.

"We've got to figure out a way to get Daisy to walk," said Jasmine.

Sofia sighed. "Yeah, she could use some motivation," she said thoughtfully. "Sometimes when I'm in the middle of a tough soccer game, I stay motivated by thinking of going out for ice cream after the game. Whenever we win, our coach treats the whole team!"

"Well, I don't think we can give a pony ice cream," Madison replied.

"No . . ." Keiko said slowly, an idea suddenly coming to her. "But we could reward her with other things she likes." Then she added, "You know, I've been thinking about something Madison said to me."

"Who, me?" Madison asked, surprised.

"Yes," Keiko said, smiling at her friend. "You told me I shouldn't give up on myself over one art contest. Well, I'm not giving up on Daisy, either!" Keiko quickly explained her plan, and her friends agreed that it was at least worth a try.

The next morning, the girls helped milk the cows and feed the chickens before heading to Grace's farm with Aunt Yumi. When they arrived, they found Marigold licking Daisy's head affectionately.

"Hi, girls," Keiko greeted the ponies. "I hope you're ready to walk today, Daisy."

"We're here to cheer you on," Madison said encouragingly as she, Sofia, and Jasmine backed up to give Keiko some space. They had agreed that they would follow Keiko's lead. Since Marigold already knew and trusted the girls, she didn't seem to mind when Keiko slowly walked Daisy out of the stall to the edge of the barn. But that's as far as Daisy would go.

The paddock in front of them was a large, oval-shaped enclosure with a high wooden fence. It was meant as a place for ponies to run and exercise, or for people to practice riding. But today Keiko's goal was to get Daisy to simply walk from one end to the other.

"I'm just going to try what Dr. Brooks showed us yesterday," Keiko explained. "If I pull Daisy's lead rope to the side so she's off-balance, hopefully she'll take a step to that side. You guys can stand nearby and spot her just in case she stumbles and starts to fall. Sound good?"

"Yes!" her friends agreed in unison.

Keiko stood next to Daisy and gently tugged the lead to one side while whispering encouraging words to the filly. At first Daisy resisted, but then she took a few wobbly steps to balance herself.

"Look, it's working!" Madison whispered excitedly.

Keiko felt a thrill of excitement. It was time for the next part of the plan.

"Do you have it, Sofia?" she asked.

Sofia nodded and showed Keiko the soft brush they had bought at the farmers market.

"Great," Keiko said. "Now remember, we'll use the brush as a reward every time Daisy takes a step."

Keiko gently pulled Daisy's lead to the side again, and the pony took a few more halting steps. When she stopped, Keiko let the pony lean against her for a moment while Sofia brushed her fluffy, soft coat.

"Nice job!" Keiko whispered softly in the filly's ear.

Next, it was Jasmine's turn. Sofia handed her the brush, and Keiko pulled the lead gently to the opposite side. Again, Daisy resisted at first. But then she took a few small, unsteady steps forward.

"Way to go, Daisy," Jasmine said encouragingly. Keiko let the pony lean against her again as Jasmine patted the filly and brushed her coat.

Once Jasmine was done brushing Daisy, she handed the brush to Madison. Keiko tugged the lead, and this time Daisy stepped forward right away, without hesitating.

"That's it, Daisy!" Madison said excitedly as she gently swiped the brush across the filly's side. "You're walking!"

Keiko smiled at her friends. True, the filly

was making progress. But would it be enough to get Daisy walking steadily on her own?

🐾 🐾 🐾

For the next two days, the girls worked patiently with Daisy every afternoon. Aunt Yumi called Grace every day with a report on how Marigold and Daisy were doing, and the girls knew Grace was hoping to avoid expensive surgery for the filly.

Dr. Brooks had been coming daily to remove the splints and check Daisy's progress. He knew the filly was improving, but he hadn't made a decision yet on whether he would have to do surgery. Today was the day of Daisy's physical exam.

Keiko and her friends hurried to Grace's

farm after their morning chores and breakfast and waited for the vet. As his truck pulled up, Keiko felt her stomach twist anxiously in anticipation.

"Hi, girls," Dr. Brooks greeted them. "Ready for Daisy's checkup?"

Keiko nodded, too nervous to talk.

"Let's see how you're doing, girl," Dr. Brooks said gently to the little filly. Then he ran his hands over her legs and made her walk across the paddock for him. The girls leaned against the fence of the paddock and watched in anticipation as Dr. Brooks led Daisy around the paddock one more time.

"She looks good, right?" Keiko asked Aunt Yumi.

Her aunt smiled proudly.

"She does," she replied.

When Dr. Brooks returned to the barn, leading the pony on her lead, he was smiling.

"She looks great," the vet reported. "Her legs are loose and limber, and she's improved a lot."

"Well?" Jasmine asked eagerly, waiting for the vet's final verdict.

"You girls did it," Dr. Brooks confirmed. "This pony is in fine shape. She's made a great recovery."

"Yay!" Keiko cried, throwing her arms around her friends in excitement. The four girls hugged each other and cheered, thrilled at the news.

Just then, they heard a truck rumbling up the road. It came to a stop next to the barn, and

Keiko saw Grace and her husband, Paul, climb out just as Dr. Brooks finished leading Daisy around the paddock.

"Is that who I think it is?" Paul asked, pointing to the filly.

"Sure is!" Keiko replied happily. "Meet Daisy!"

Grace let out a happy laugh as she came closer to the paddock, following the foal's every movement.

"I can't believe how well she's doing!" Grace exclaimed. "This doesn't look like a filly who will need surgery, that's for sure."

"That must be a relief to you," Aunt Yumi said, squeezing her friend's arm.

Dr. Brooks cleared his throat. "You have these young ladies to thank," he said. "They came every day and worked patiently with the pony. They never gave up on her. And somehow they managed to keep Marigold happy at the same time."

Grace turned to the girls and smiled. "I'm so grateful."

Keiko beamed. She was thrilled that Daisy had improved so much, and she was especially glad to have helped Grace.

Jasmine nudged Keiko forward. "Actually," she said, "it was Keiko who first figured out that Marigold was in labor."

"She's the one who came up with the idea we used to get the foal to walk, which helped her legs heal," Sofia agreed.

"She even came up with the perfect name for her!" Madison added.

Keiko, blushing from all the praise, looked up at Grace. "I hope you like the name Daisy."

"Like it?" Grace replied. "It's perfect! Thank you so much."

Keiko turned to watch Daisy trotting beside Marigold, a springy step in her long legs. "You're welcome," Keiko replied happily.

Chapter 10
New Arrivals

The girls were fast asleep when Aunt Yumi came upstairs to wake them on their last morning at Cherry Blossom Farm.

"Is it time to get up already?" Keiko whispered, rubbing her eyes.

Her aunt laughed. "I'm afraid so," she replied. "But it's your last day of rising early, so let's make the most of it. I have a surprise for all of you, so get dressed and meet me near the henhouse. And bring your sketchbook, Keiko!"

The odd request got Keiko's attention. She forced herself out of bed and shook the others awake.

The girls dressed quickly, put on their shoes, and headed outside.

"Aunt Yumi?" Keiko called from outside the hen coop.

"I'm in here!" The girls heard Aunt Yumi's voice from inside.

When Keiko and her friends entered the tiny building, everything looked the same at first. Keiko saw the usual line of hens perched on their nests. But something sounded different. There were high-pitched chirping sounds coming from a small box at the other end of the coop.

Aunt Yumi turned to the girls and

whispered, "Marigold isn't the only new mom around here. The chicks finally hatched last night!"

Madison let out an involuntary squeal. Sure enough, five tiny, fuzzy yellow chicks were snuggled in a heap of pine shavings. Keiko loved how bright they were against the brown pine shavings, like little balls of butter. She immediately wanted to sketch them.

"Oh my gosh, they're adorable!" Jasmine said in a loud whisper.

"Can we hold them?" Keiko asked her aunt.

"As long as you're careful," Aunt Yumi replied. She lifted one chick and placed it in Keiko's open palm, showing her how to gently hold the wings in place against the chick's body. Aunt Yumi gave a chick to each girl.

"It's so soft!" Madison exclaimed in surprise.

"And light," whispered Sofia as she carefully petted her chick on its back with one finger.

"This is so cool," Jasmine said in awe.

When they had put all the chicks back in the box and quietly left the chicken coop, Keiko glanced up at her aunt.

"Isn't it time for us to feed the hens?" she asked.

"Not today," Aunt Yumi replied. "It's your last day here, so your uncle and I will take care of the chores. But there's one last thing I haven't had a chance to show you girls yet. Follow me!"

Aunt Yumi led the girls past the barn to a tall tree. A small tree house was wedged between its branches like a shoebox, and a rope ladder dangled down the side.

"From that tree house, you can see the whole farm," said Aunt Yumi. "I figured you girls would like to climb up and take one last look before you go. And I thought Keiko might want to do one last sketch before she goes."

Keiko took a deep breath. "Okay," she said softly. "But you know I didn't win the contest, right?" Keiko was sure her uncle had told Aunt Yumi the news.

"You can try again next year," Aunt Yumi responded. "You can't give up so quickly. Skill takes practice. After all, what would Daisy have done if you had given up on her?"

Keiko's friends nodded in agreement.

"Will you guys stay with me?" Keiko asked.

"Of course!" cried Madison.

And with that, the girls climbed up into the tree house to enjoy the beautiful farm one last time, from above.

🐾 🐾 🐾

Later that morning, after the girls had milked Buttercup and Lulu for the last time, Keiko, Sofia, Madison, and Jasmine headed over to Grace's farm to say good-bye to Marigold and Daisy. The ponies trotted right over to the fence and nuzzled the girls happily.

Then Keiko pulled her sketchbook out of her backpack and tore out a single page. "I wanted you to have this," she said, handing the drawing to Grace.

It was the picture she had drawn of Marigold and Daisy, just after the filly was born. "Oh, it's beautiful!" Grace cried. "You're a wonderful artist. I love it."

Keiko smiled as she watched Daisy trot around the paddock one last time. Her heart felt full. She was so glad to have people around who believed in her, like her best friends, Aunt Yumi, and Grace. And she knew she would remember this summer for a long time to come.

Don't miss the next **forever friends** book!

Sofia's Puppy Love

Sofia has wanted a dog for as long as she can remember, but her parents have been reluctant. But when a litter of puppies is born at the animal shelter, Sofia's mom says they might be able to adopt one—*if* Sofia can prove she can take care of it, that is. Sofia is sure she can prove herself. But then one thing after another goes wrong. Will Sofia's dream of owning a dog ever come true?

Meet
Luciana Vega!

Luciana Vega is always reaching for the stars.
Her dream is to be the first kid on Mars. But will her
dreams get in the way of finding true friendships?